Goodnight Josie

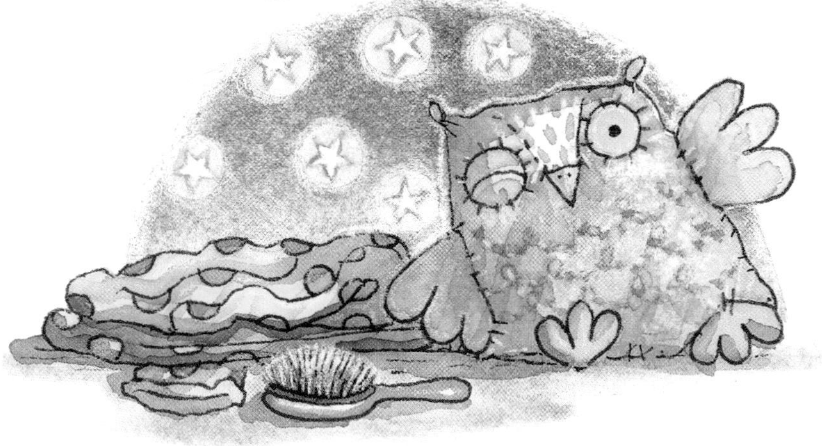

Alison Hawes
Illustrated by Lisa Smith

RIGBY

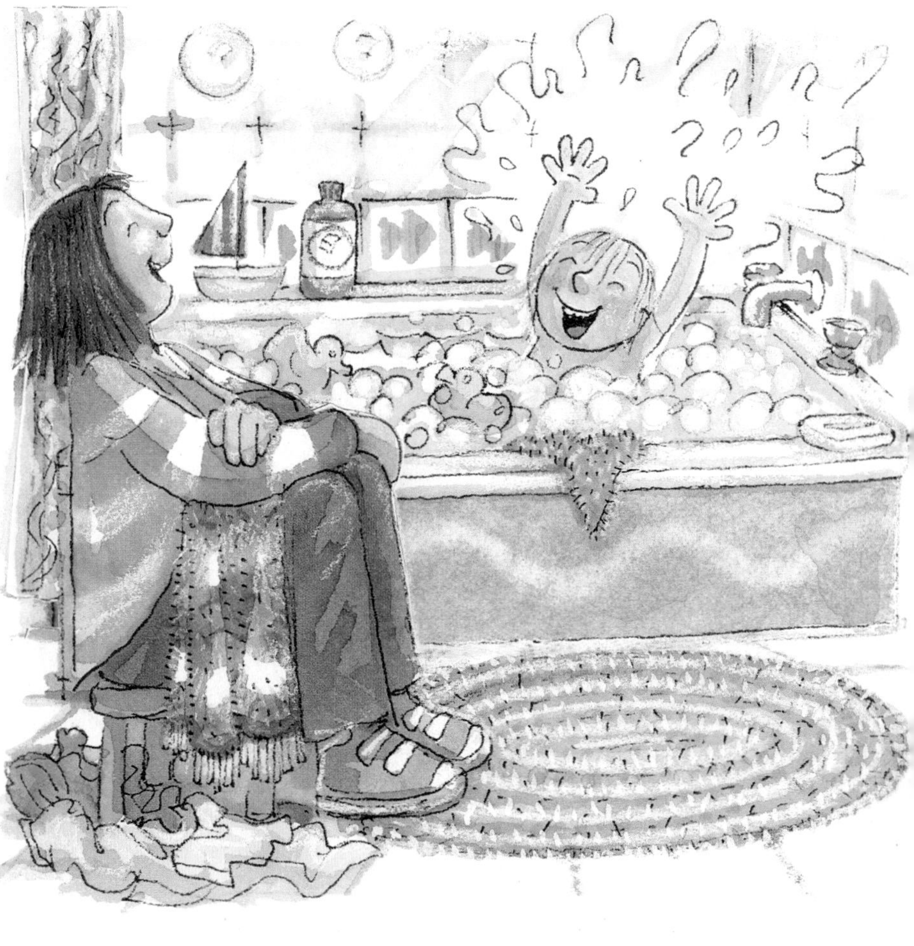

my bath

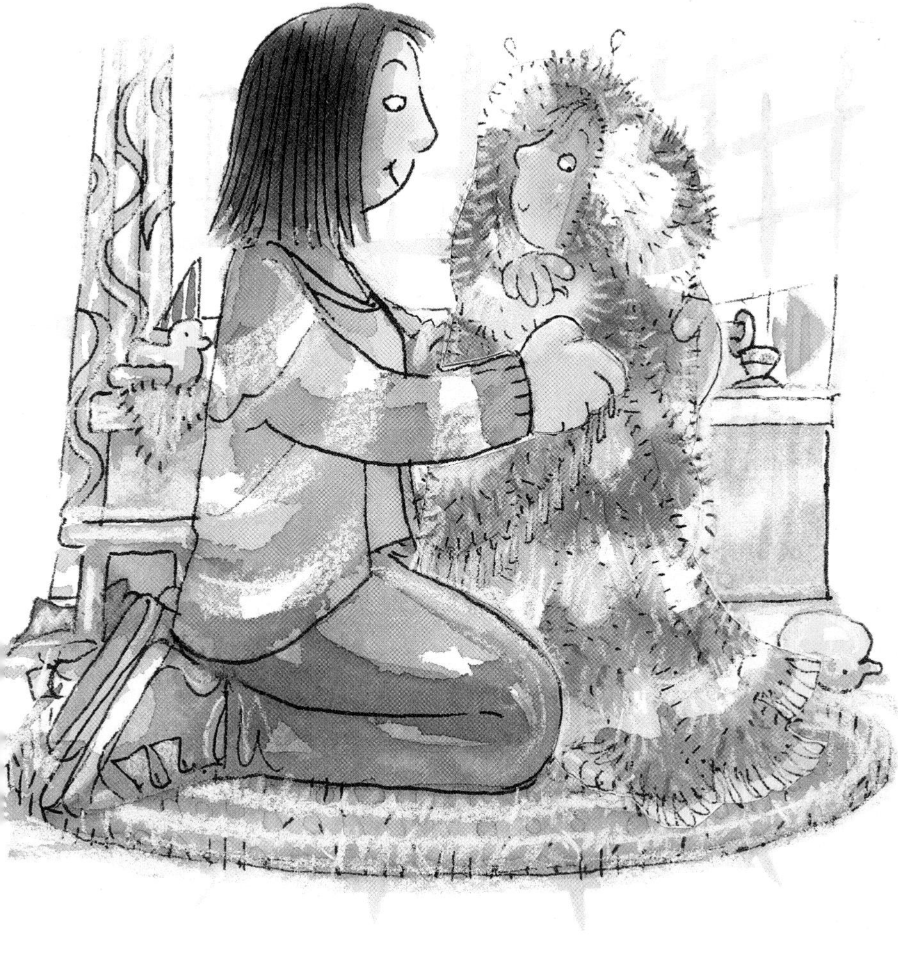

my towel

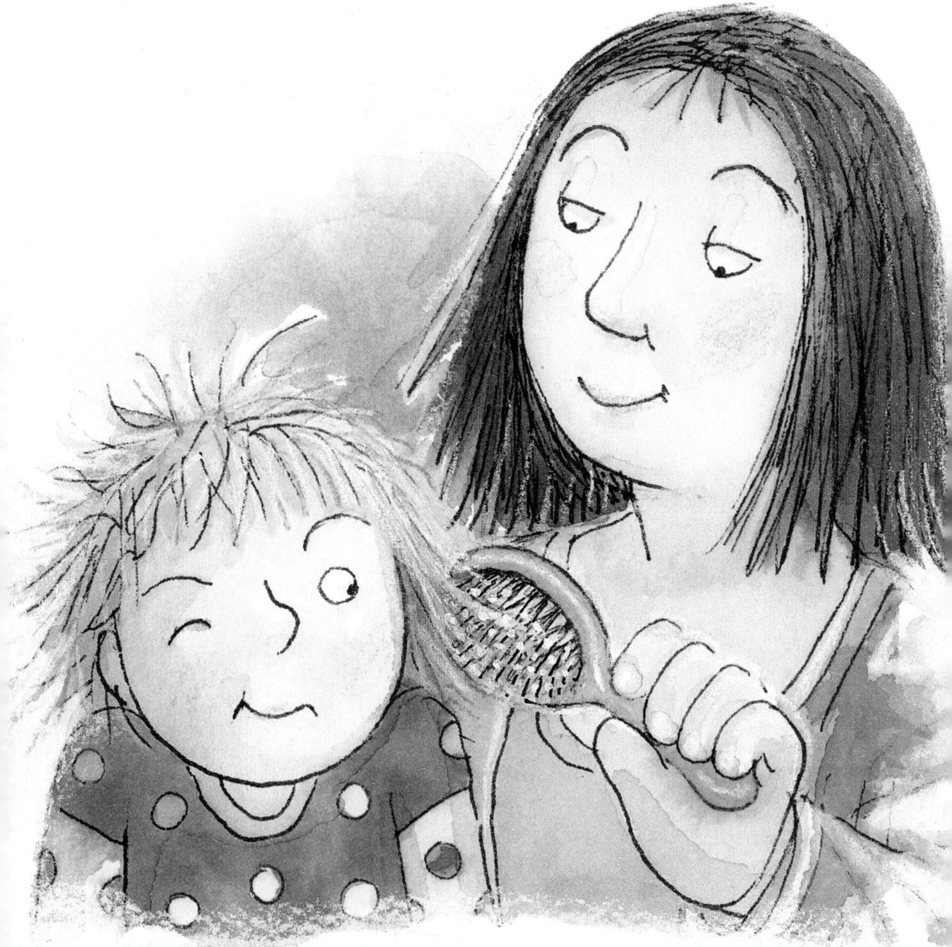

my brush

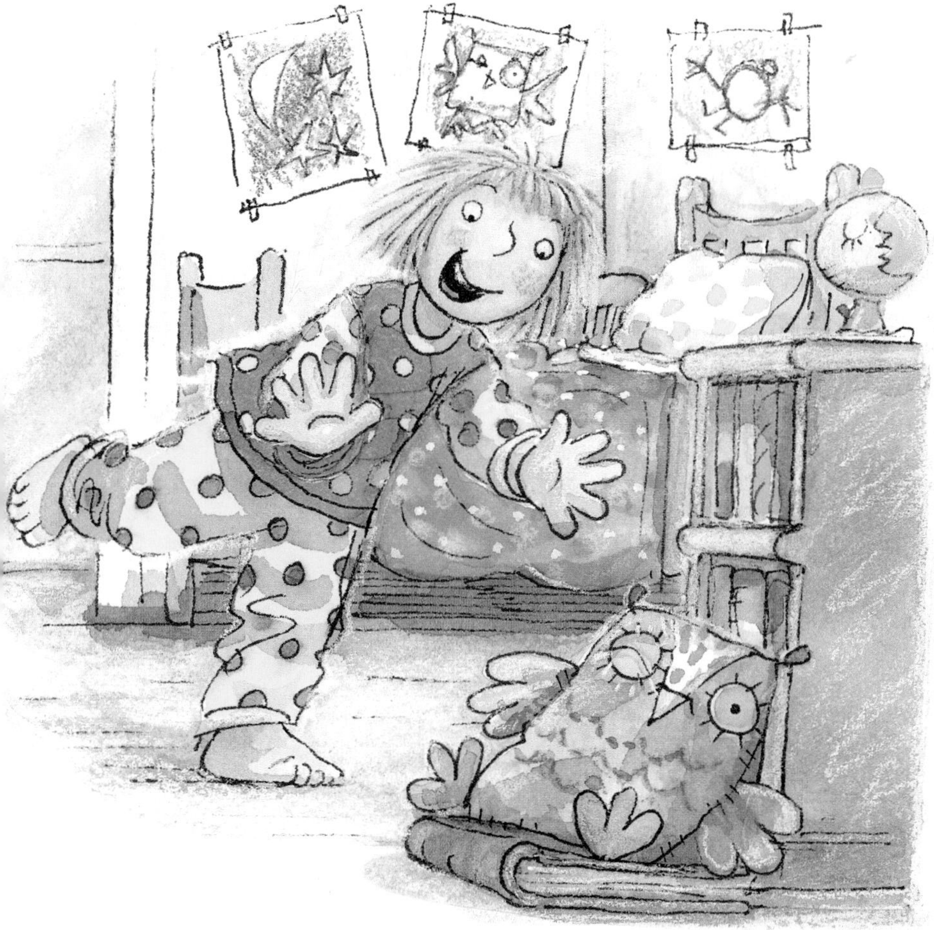

my owl

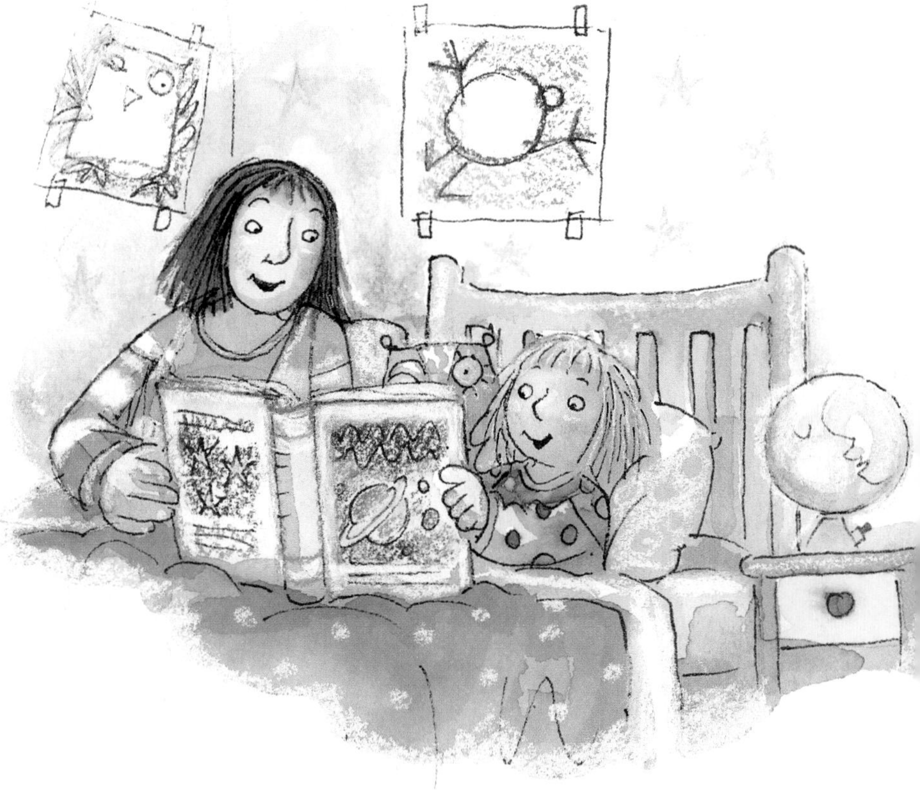

my book

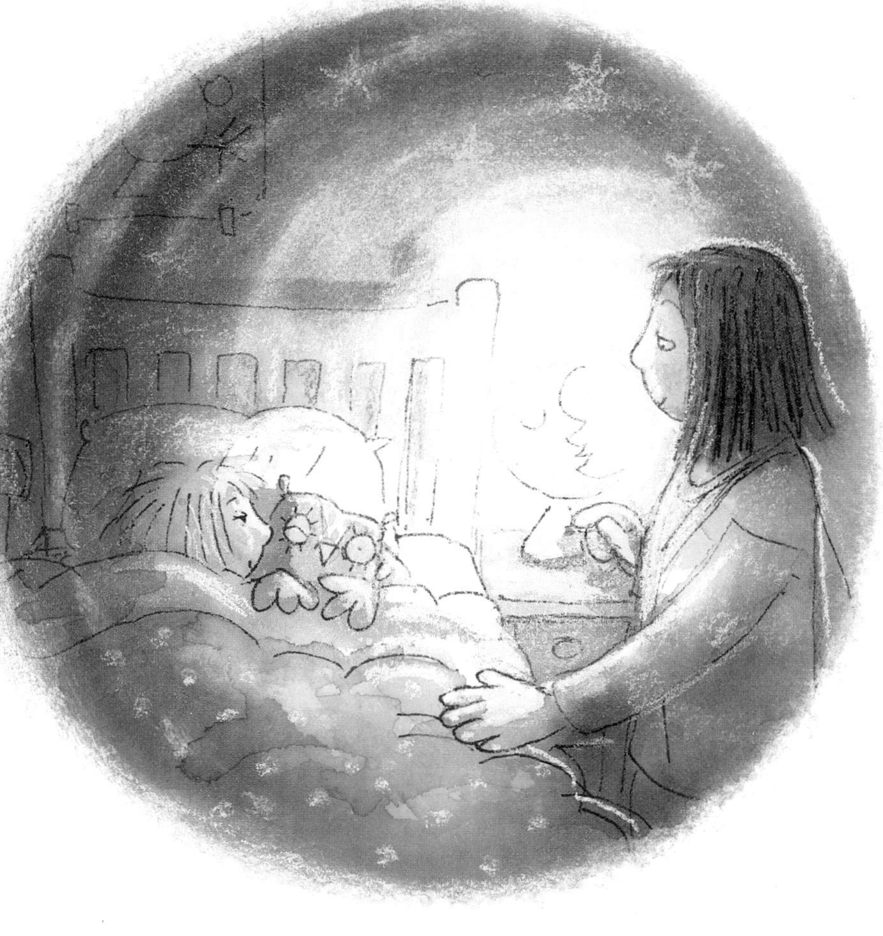

my light

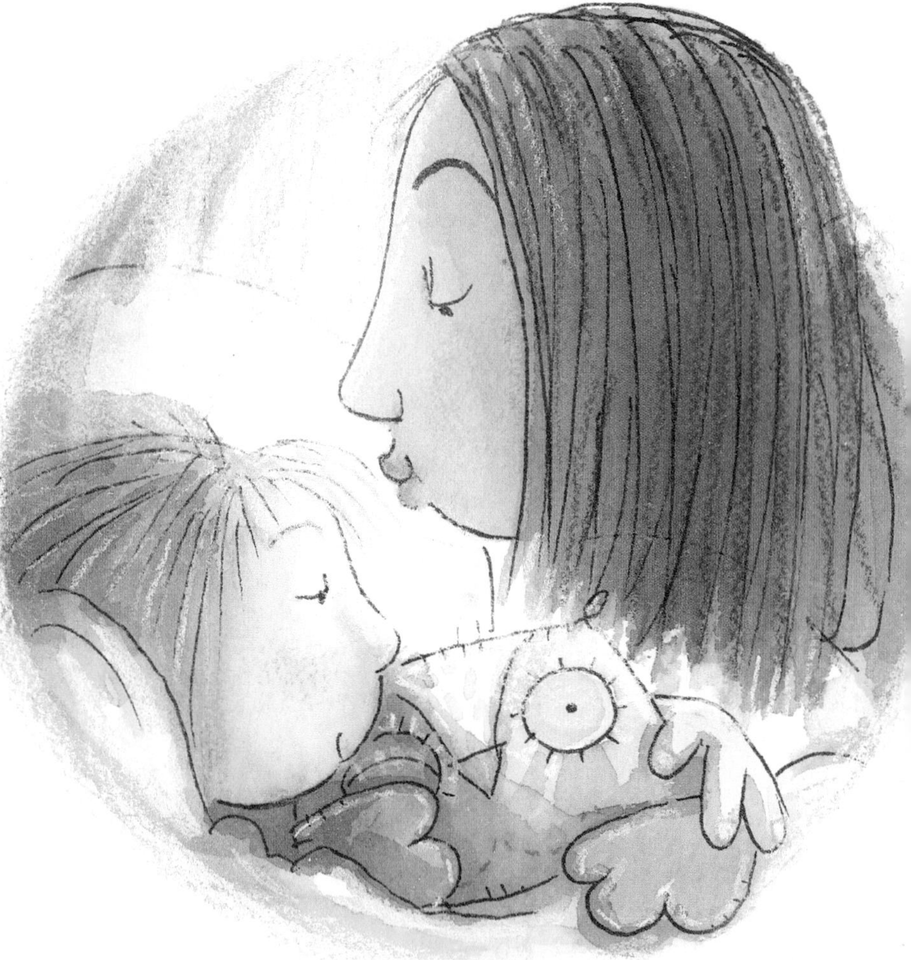

my kiss goodnight